W9-DCM-474

DISGUST   ANGER   FEAR

To Madeline,
whose endlessly
fascinating Mind World
dazzles me every day.
—Love, Mom

For my girls: Julie, Emma,
Libby, and Lolly.
—Dan

Copyright © 2015 Disney Enterprises, Inc., and Pixar Animation Studios. All rights reserved. Published by Disney Press, an imprint of Disney Book Group. No part of this book may be reproduced or transmitted in any form or by any means, electronic or mechanical, including photocopying, recording, or by any information storage and retrieval system, without written permission from the publisher. For information address Disney Press, 1101 Flower Street, Glendale, California 91201.
Printed in the United States
First Hardcover Edition, May 2015
10 9 8 7 6 5 4 3 2 1
F322-8368-0-15079
ISBN 978-1-4847-1280-1
Library of Congress Control Number: 2014954372
Visit www.disneybooks.com

Disney·PIXAR
INSIDE OUT

Sadly Ever After?

by **Elise Allen**

illustrated by Daniel Holland

Disney PRESS
Los Angeles · New York

This is Riley. Isn't she amazing? She lives in Minnesota and is great at doing lots of things—like skating. Look how fast she can go!

We did lots of things that day. We played Frisbee . . .

I feel *sad*. We wanted to take that dog home, but Mom and Dad wouldn't let us.

Remember when we were making a daisy chain? A giant bee flew out of the grass and nearly stung us in the face! *Wasn't that horrifying?*

It makes me furious! That bus driver left three seconds early that day!

And we nearly choked to death on the bus exhaust! **So** beyond gross.

It was like being trapped in a horror movie! AND we were going to get in trouble for being late to school!

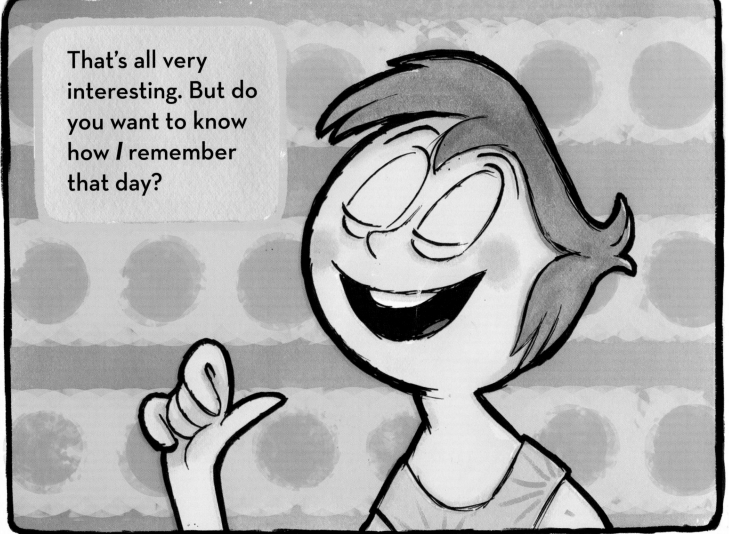

That's all very interesting. But do you want to know how *I* remember that day?

Mom ended up driving us to school. We sang out loud to the radio and even stopped for hot chocolate! Don't you remember how amazing it was?

You're right, Joy. Maybe that wasn't so bad.

Who could be grossed out by hot chocolate?

I feel all warm and cozy and safe now.